BOOKTOPUS

Busy FARM Activity Book

Amazing book for amazing kids!

Colour the picture with your favourite colours.

Match each animal to its shadow.

Trace the path and help the goat reach the flowers.

Write the name of the given farm animals.

Trace the path and help the chick reach the hen.

Colour the picture beautifully.

Trace the pattern in each row.

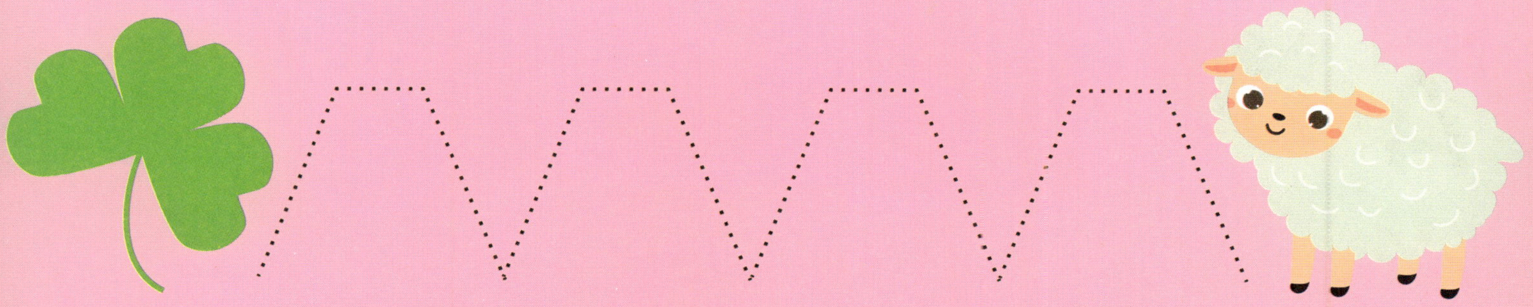

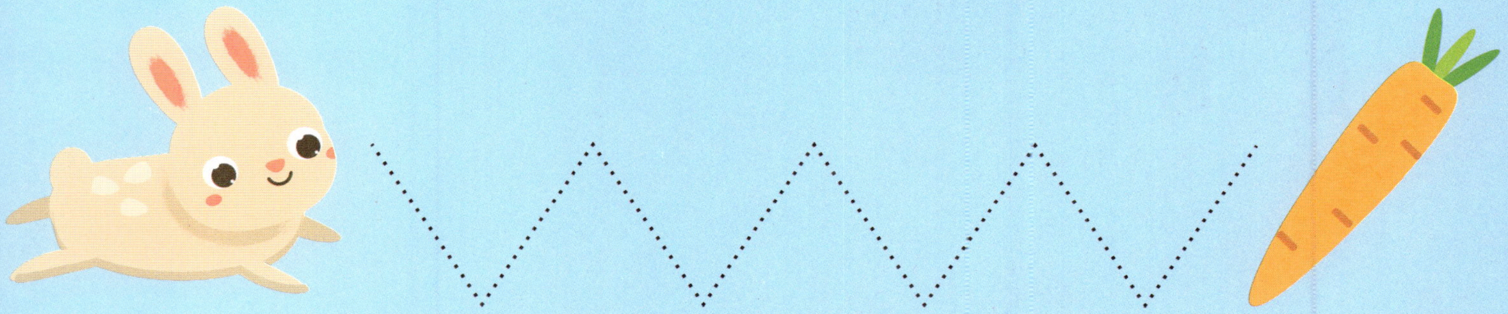

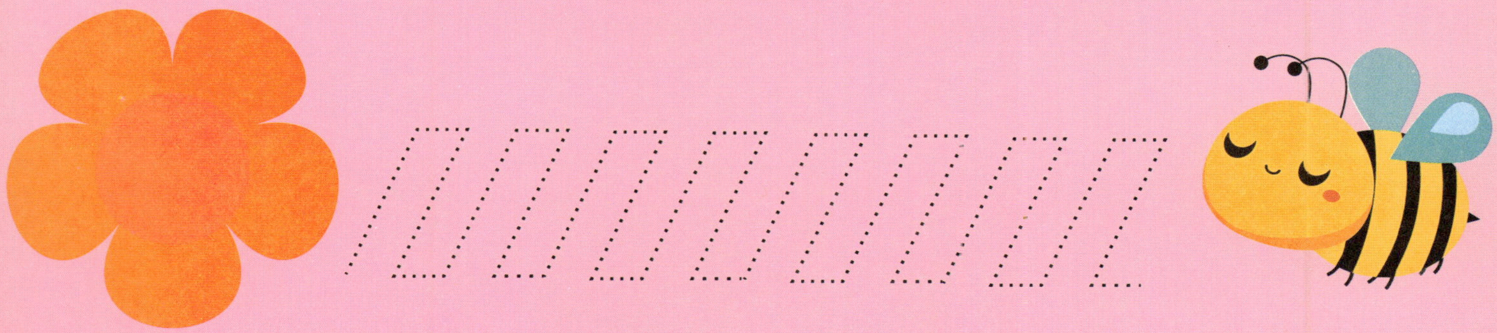

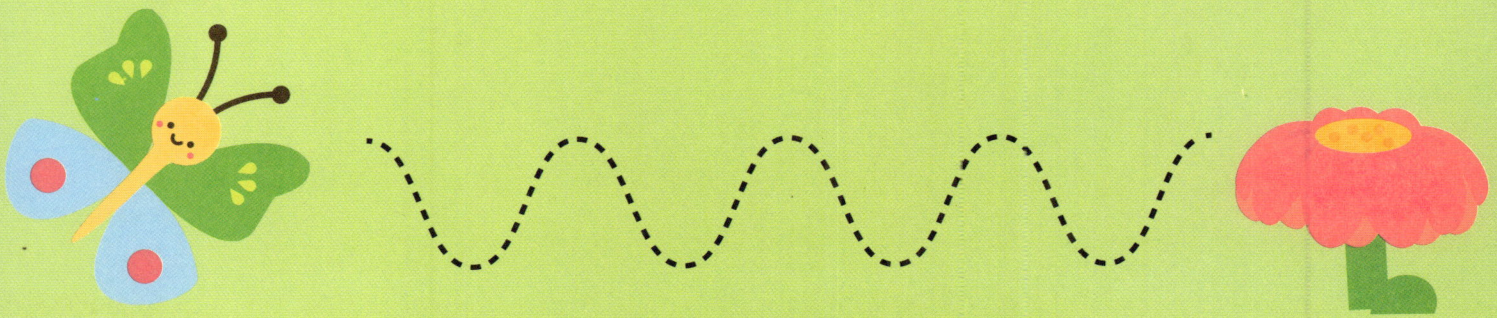

What comes next? Place the alphabet of the animal in each blank space.

Look carefully and circle the pig that looks different.

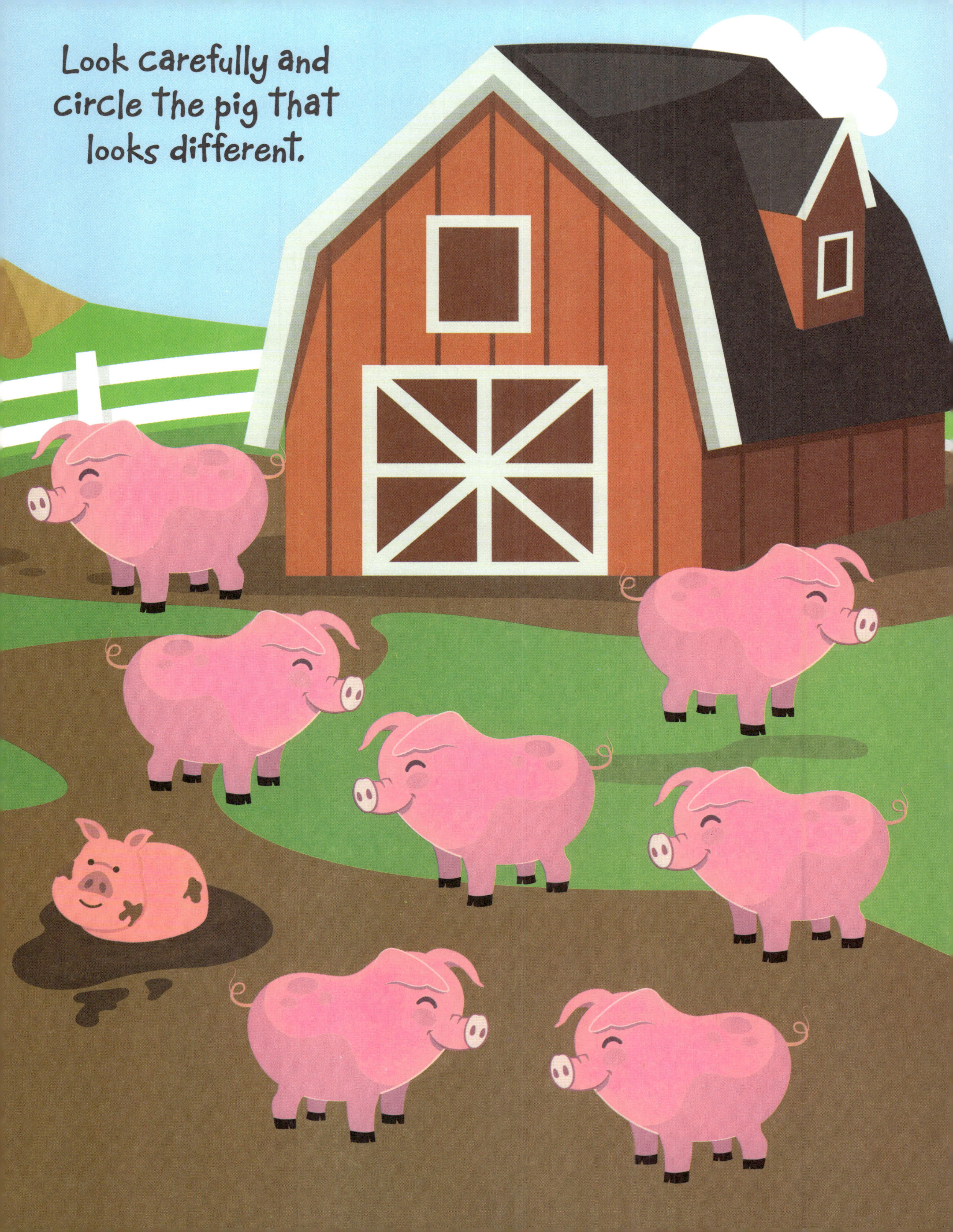

Circle the differences between the two pictures given below.

Count and write how many times each vegetable is appearing below.

Follow the steps and draw the sheep.

Write the name of this farm object and circle its correct shadow.

Follow the duck's footprints and help it reach the pumpkin.

Find the correct shadows of the animals and write the corresponding numbers on them.

Count and write how many times each animal is appearing below.

Connect the dots and colour the picture.

Draw and Colour the pig as shown.

Trace the correct string to help the chick find its mom.

Write the name of the given farm objects.

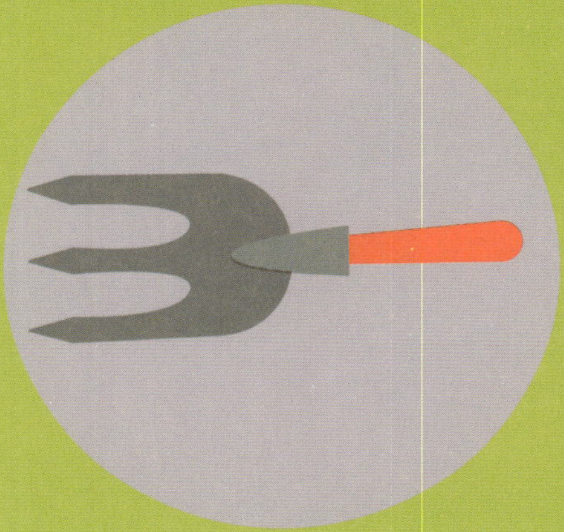

Match each farm animal to the product they give.

Number the chicks that look the same from 1 to 4 in the given columns. One is done for you.

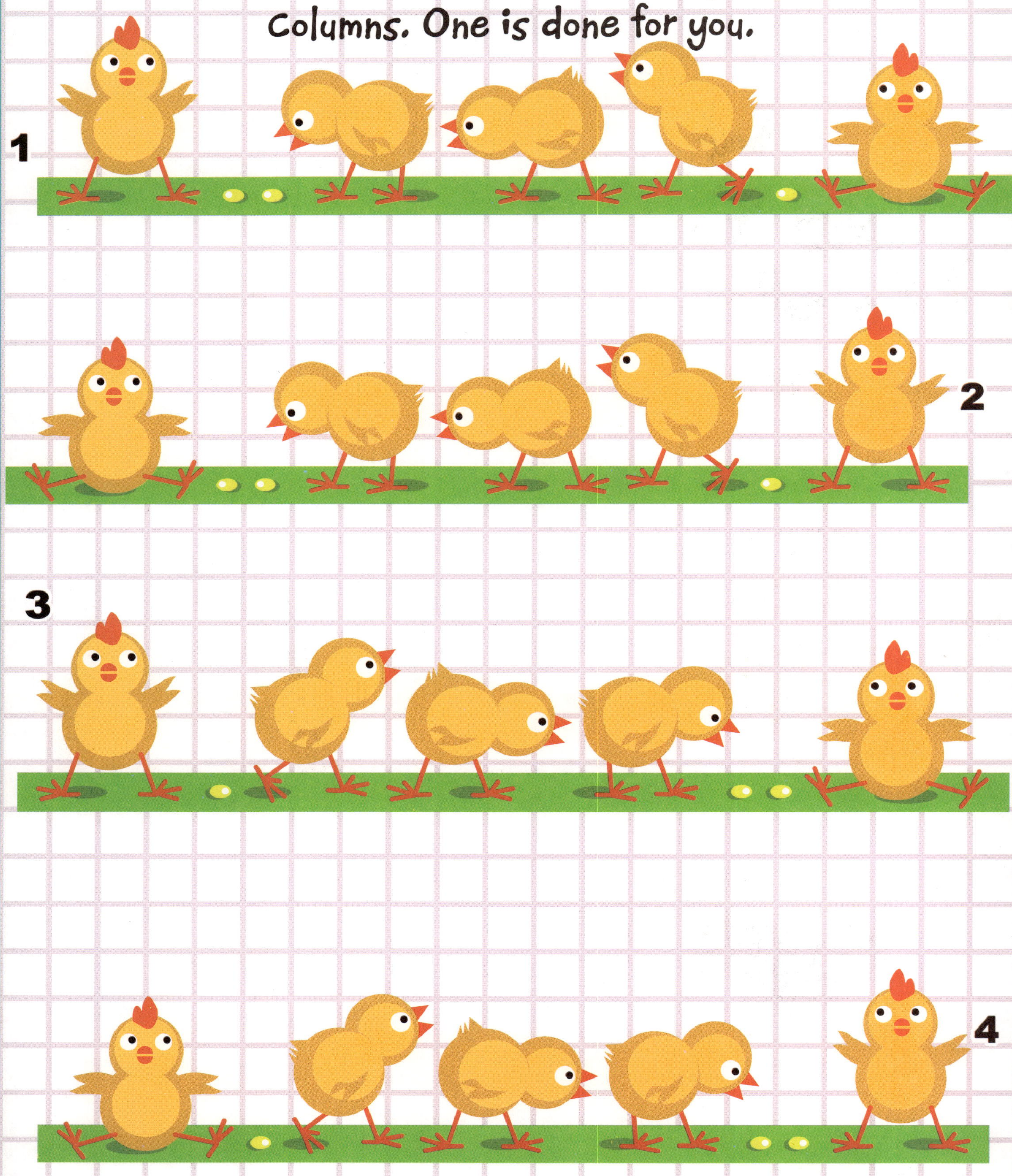

Find the missing piece of the picture.

Write the correct answer.

1

2

3

Colour the picture beautifully.

Help the farmer reach the barn.

Help the farmer sort these crops by writing 'F' for fruits and 'V' for vegetables.

Circle the differences in these two pictures.

Circle the identical ducks.

Match each animal to its home.

Tick the missing piece of the puzzle.

Find and circle 10 bees in the garden.

Count and write how many are facing left and how many are facing right.

left

right

Busy FARM Activity Book

BOOKTOPUS
An imprint of HarperCollins *Publishers* India
www.harpercollins.co.in
HarperCollinsIN

BOOKTOPUS

Mighty DINOSAURS Activity Book

49
+ 34

Amazing book for amazing kids!

Trace the lines and colour the eggs as shown.

How many dinos are facing to the left ?
How many are facing to the right?

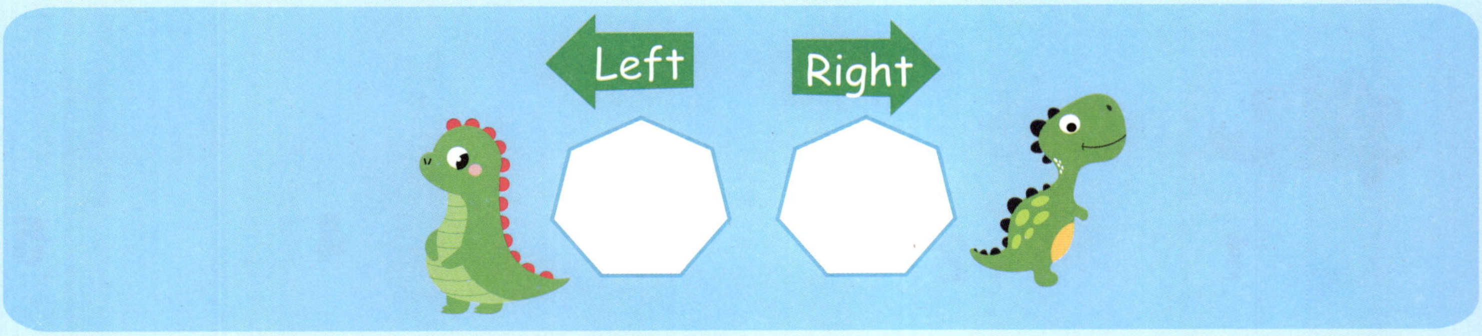

Who comes next? Place the correct number in the given space in each row.

Colour the picture in bright colours.

Connect the dots and colour the dinosaur.

Solve the addition sums and write the answers.

$$\begin{array}{r} 4\ 9 \\ +\ 3\ 4 \\ \hline \end{array}$$

$$\begin{array}{r} 2\ 5 \\ +\ 2\ 0 \\ \hline \end{array}$$

$$\begin{array}{r} 3\ 5 \\ +\ 9\ 2 \\ \hline \end{array}$$

$$\begin{array}{r} 4\ 6 \\ +\ 3\ 2 \\ \hline \end{array}$$

$$\begin{array}{r} 5\ 9 \\ +\ 6\ 7 \\ \hline \end{array}$$

Match each dino to its other half.

Count and write how many times each dino is appearing below.

Draw and Colour the dino as shown.

Find the path to help mama dino reach her baby.

Circle the differences in the two pictures given below.

Write the number of the correct missing piece on the empty circle.

1

2

3

Look carefully and circle the two different dinos.

Colour the picture with your favourite colours.

Count the objects in each row and match to your answer.

7

5

4

2

3

6

Match each dino to its baby.

Count and write the total number of bones.

There are

Bones.

Trace the lines.

Circle the correct shadow of the given dino.

Look carefully at all the objects, and tick the smallest object you see in each row.

Count and write how many times each dino is appearing below.

Match each dino to its shadow.

Colour the picture by following the coloured dots.

Spot the dinos given below in the picture.

Match each egg to its missing part.

Circle the dino that looks different in each row.

Solve the subtraction sums.

$$\begin{array}{r} 89 \\ -\ 31 \\ \hline \end{array}$$

$$\begin{array}{r} 58 \\ -\ 12 \\ \hline \end{array}$$

$$\begin{array}{r} 45 \\ -\ 43 \\ \hline \end{array}$$

$$\begin{array}{r} 87 \\ -\ 61 \\ \hline \end{array}$$

$$\begin{array}{r} 89 \\ -\ 78 \\ \hline \end{array}$$

Find the path to help mama dino reach her baby.

Match each dino to its shadow.

Count the objects and circle your answer in each box.

2	5	3

7	2	1

6	1	5

9	4	3

Trace the path and help each dino get to its egg.

Circle the things that are not related to dinos.

Mighty DINOSAURS Activity Book

BOOKTOPUS
An imprint of HarperCollins *Publishers* India
www.harpercollins.co.in
HarperCollinsIN

BOOKTOPUS

Magical UNICORNS Activity Book

Amazing book for amazing kids!

Match each unicorn to its horseshoe.

How many stars do you see? Write in the box.

Match each unicorn to its other half.

Circle the cupcake identical to the cupcake the unicorn likes.

Spot and circle the given pictures in the scene.

Solve the addition sums and write the answers.

$$\begin{array}{r} 4\ 9 \\ +\ 3\ 4 \\ \hline \end{array}$$

$$\begin{array}{r} 2\ 5 \\ +\ 2\ 0 \\ \hline \end{array}$$

$$\begin{array}{r} 3\ 5 \\ +\ 9\ 2 \\ \hline \end{array}$$

$$\begin{array}{r} 4\ 6 \\ +\ 3\ 2 \\ \hline \end{array}$$

$$\begin{array}{r} 5\ 9 \\ +\ 6\ 7 \\ \hline \end{array}$$

Draw and Colour the unicorn as shown.

Draw expressions on the unicorn faces.

I feel
Happy

I feel
Sad

I feel
in Love

I feel
Angry

Circle the smallest object in each row.

Add the objects and tick the correct answer in each box.

4 9 3

7 4 1

2 1 5

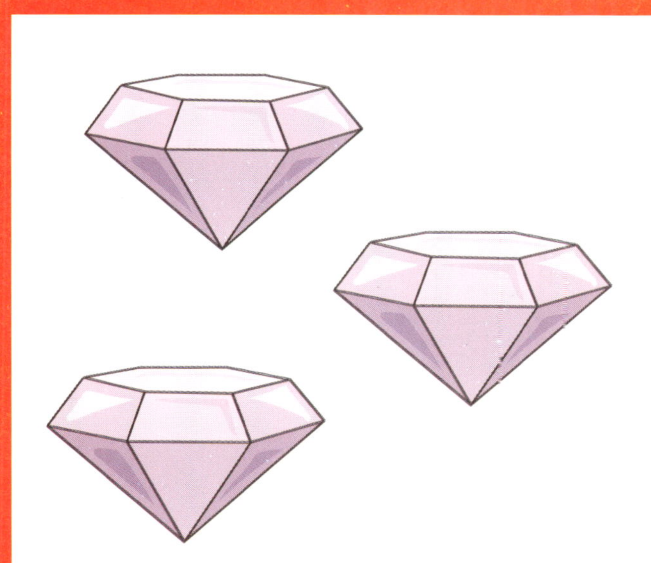

5 4 3

Circle the odd one out.

Trace, draw and colour the object in each row.

Follow the given colour code to colour the picture.

1 3 5

2 4 6

Trace the lines.

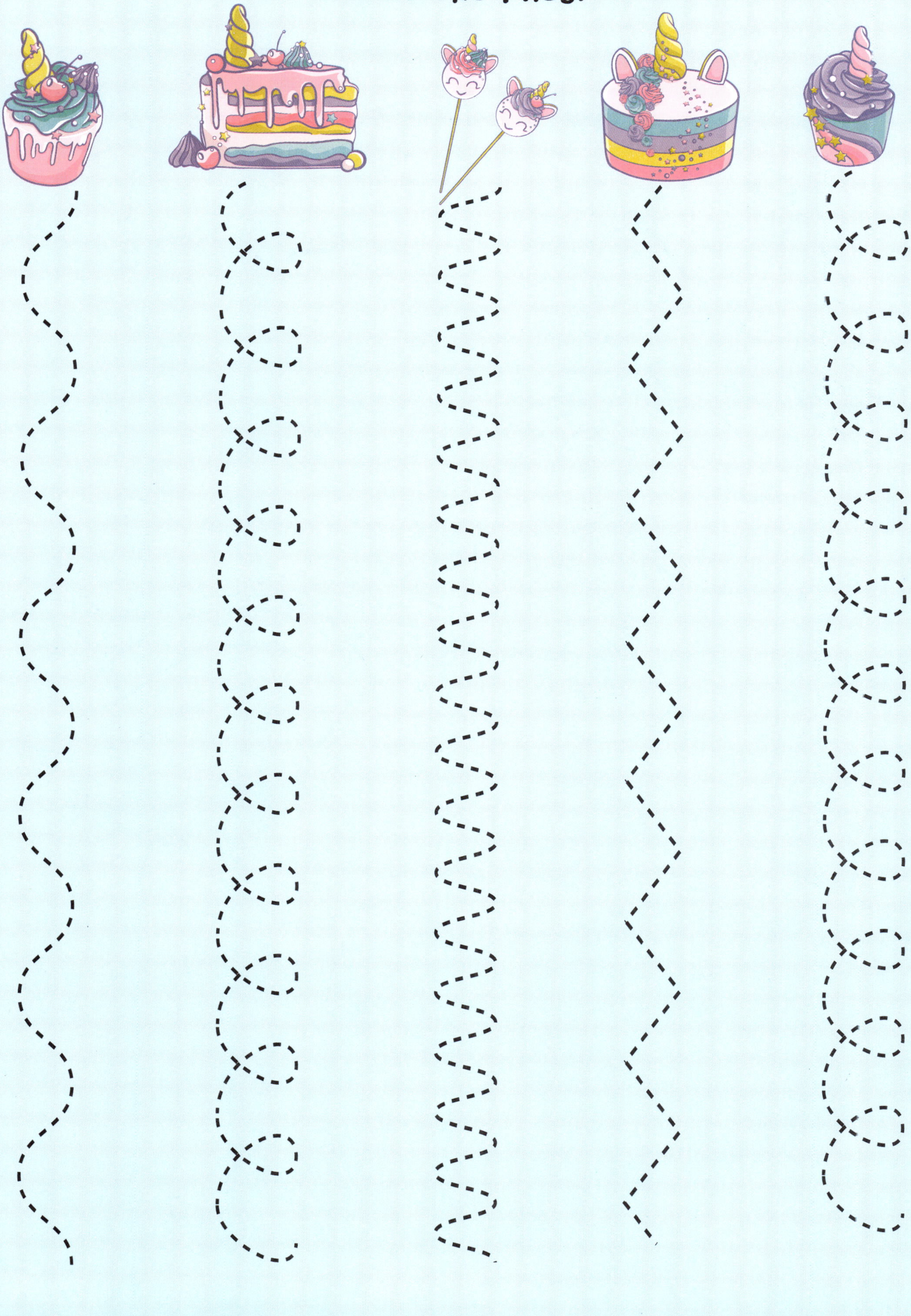

Connect the dots and colour the unicorn.

How many unicorns are facing to the right and how many are facing to the left?

← Left	→ Right

Circle the biggest picture in each row.

Match each unicorn to its shadow.

Help the unicorn collect all the doughnuts in a single take without repeating the path twice.

Colour the picture and write the total number of stars and clouds.

Clouds ☐

Stars ☐

Help the unicorn find the rainbow.

What comes next? Tick the correct option in each column.

Trace the path through the clouds to take the unicorn to the rainbow.

Spot 10 differences.

How many unicorns do you see?

Solve the picture sums by following the given code.

Colour the magic elements.

Spot and circle the differences between these two pictures.

Connect the dots and colour the unicorn.

Look carefully and circle the two different unicorns.

Circle the object that only appears once in the grid.

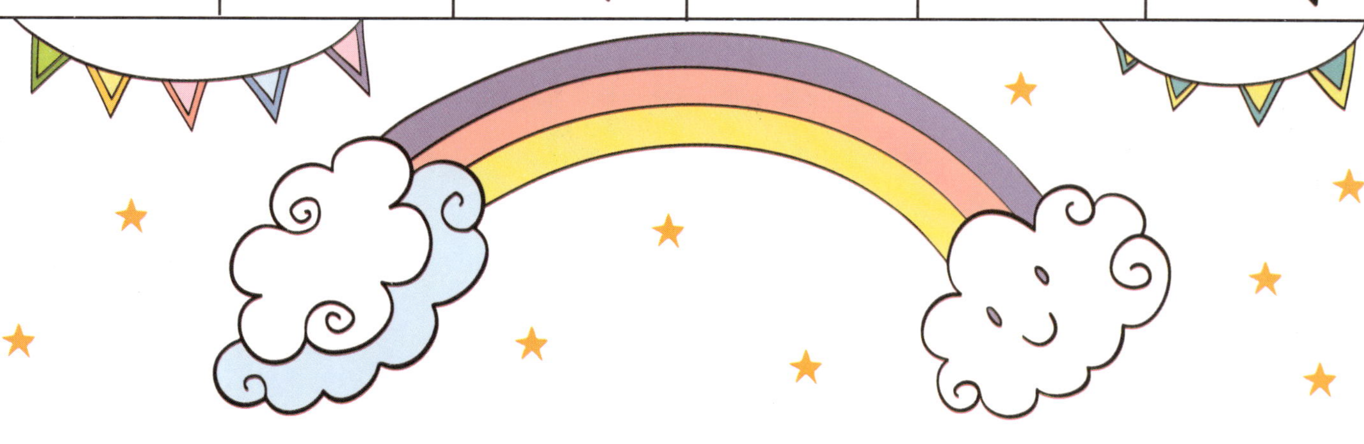

Count and write how many times each object is appearing below.

Trace the paths and circle the unicorn that will get the magic wand.

Magical UNICORNS Activity Book

BOOKTOPUS
An imprint of HarperCollins *Publishers* India
www.harpercollins.co.in
HarperCollinsIN